Little Things

Written by Scott M. Huse
Illustrated by Janice Northcutt Huse

Little Things
Copyright © 2002 by Scott M. Huse
Published by MorningStar Fellowship Church
P.O. Box 19409, Charlotte, NC 28219-9409

International Standard Book Number 1-929371-21-7
MorningStar's Website: www.morningstarministries.org
For information call 800-542-0278

ong, long ago in a faraway land high atop a mountain there lived a happy little family. Normally their lives were quiet and peaceful, but not today.

immy and Amber's mother rushed into their room very early in the morning calling, "Wake up! Wake up! The King is coming to town today and we have to hurry and get ready."

Although the sun was only just beginning to rise, Timmy and Amber were eager to get up and get ready. They knew how much fun they would have at the festival for the King.

here would be horse rides, pie eating contests, races, prizes, music, and archery contests. They might even get to see the King! They could hardly wait. But before they could go, they would have to clean their room.

o they worked very hard together cleaning their room. They put away all their toys, clothes, and books. They made their beds and swept the floor. Finally, they were all done.

immy and Amber sat down exhausted from all their hard work. While they were resting, Amber saw something on the floor. "What's that?" she asked. "Oh, that's just a little marble; it doesn't matter," said Timmy.

uddenly the little marble went flying! Their pet cat, Spunky, jumped down and started batting the marble around. It crashed off the wall and zoomed right out of their room!!

own the stairs the little marble flew and out the front door it bounced. Spunky was chasing right behind it, and Timmy and Amber were running right behind Spunky!

ust outside there was a messenger boy who was delivering important papers. He slipped on the marble and fell right to the ground. "Ouch!" said the boy in a very loud voice. When he fell, all the papers he was carrying went flying everywhere!

ust then, a knight on a huge white horse was passing by. All of the excitement and the flying papers frightened the horse terribly. He took off running very fast and was completely out of control!

he knight cried out, "Whoa boy, whoa!" but it was no use. The terrified horse raced through gardens, through storefronts, and through flower beds breaking everything in sight. Then, the horse crashed right into a gigantic pile of watermelons!

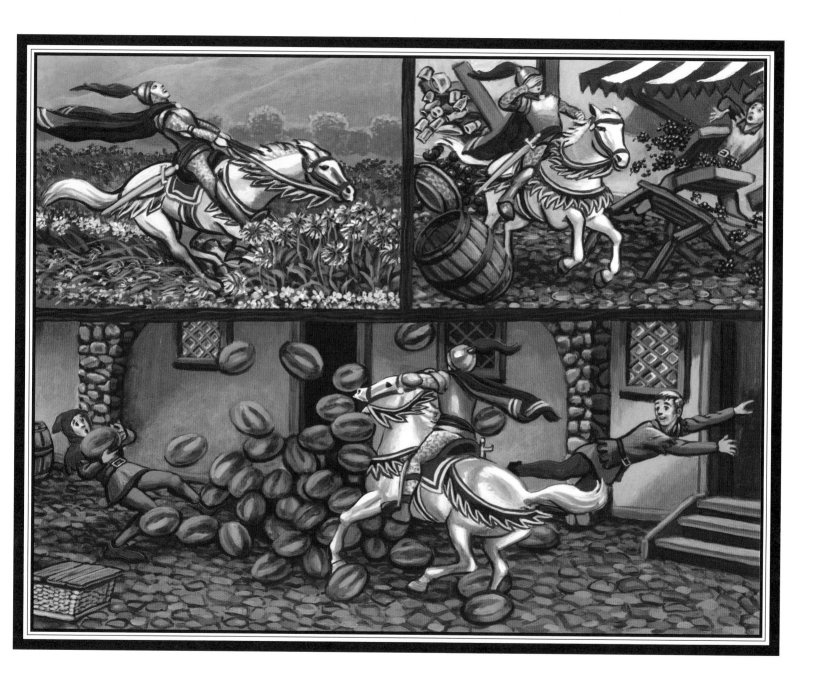

own the hill the watermelons raced, rolling faster and faster as they sped along. Some crashed right through windows. Others flew into crowds, knocking people down and causing panic in the streets.

Some of the watermelons raced down a hill and out into the countryside. As they bumped into rocks, they bounced up and flew into the air. One even hit a bull right on the head! finally, all the watermelons stopped rolling—all except for one little watermelon, that is.

That one little watermelon continued rolling all the way to the edge of a cliff where it bumped into a giant boulder. The boulder was on the very edge of the cliff overlooking the valley below. It was right above the town where the King was just about to arrive.

he giant boulder, which had been there for as long as anyone could remember, gave way. It plunged down the mountainside crashing into trees and bushes, destroying everything in its path.

aster and faster it rolled causing other rocks and boulders to break loose too. A very dangerous avalanche was now racing toward the unsuspecting town below.

uddenly someone screamed, "HELP! Run for your lives!!" But it was too late. The avalanche of huge boulders and rocks was already upon them. There was no time to escape. Even the King, who had just arrived, was doomed!

One of Timmy's friends standing nearby panicked and started shaking him saying "What can we do? What can we do?!

s he was being shaken, Timmy awoke to hear Amber say, "Wake up. Wake up, Timmy. It's time to go now." Timmy suddenly realized that it had all just been a terrible dream!

immy ran over to the little marble, picked it up, and put it right where it belonged. He now knew that even little things can cause big problems if they are not taken care of right away. On the way to the festival, Timmy told Amber the whole dream. She thought it was very exciting and a good lesson to learn.

ater that day at the festival, they had the best time of their lives. They won prizes, rode horses, shot arrows, and they even got to see the King! It was a day of fun they would always remember and a great lesson about little things that they would never forget.